To dear Maxime,
with love from
Godmother Mary.

(SEE P. 18) *'No, there, my dear,' said the queen*

TALES FROM ANDERSEN

Translated by *W. K. Holmes*
and illustrated by *Barbara Freeman*

BLACKIE: LONDON AND GLASGOW

THIS IS THE FIRST PART
OF A COLLECTION OF TALES FROM
ANDERSEN AND GRIMM

Blackie & Son Ltd., 5 Fitzhardinge Street, London, W.1
17 Stanhope Street, Glasgow
Blackie & Son (India) Ltd., Bombay; Blackie & Son (Canada) Ltd., Toronto

Printed in Great Britain by Blackie & Son, Ltd., Glasgow

Contents

TALES FROM ANDERSEN

(H70)

THE TINDER-BOX

A soldier was marching along a country road—left, right; left, right! His knapsack was on his back and his sword by his side, for he was on his way home from the wars.

On his way he met a horrible-looking old witch. She said to him, 'Good evening, soldier! What a fine sword you have and what a big knapsack! A proper soldier you are! And you can have as much money as you want.'

'Thanks, old witch!' said the soldier.

'Do you see that big tree?' said the witch, pointing to an oak at the roadside. 'It is hollow. Climb up it till you find a hole. Get in through that and

'Climb up till you find a hole'

8

(SEE P. 10)

All those candles were burning

climb down. I'll tie a rope round your waist and pull you up when you call.'

'And what am I to do when I'm in there?' asked the soldier.

'Get money!' said the witch. 'Listen; when you get right down you'll find yourself in a hall, lit with more than a hundred candles. You will see three doors. You can open them, for the keys are in the locks. If you go through the first door you'll find yourself in a room where there is a big chest lying on the floor. On it is sitting a dog with eyes as big as saucers, but you won't have any trouble with him. I'll give you my blue apron; spread it on the floor, pick up the dog quickly, put him on my apron, then open the chest and take as much money as you like. It is all in coppers.

'If you'd rather have silver, you must go into the next room. There is a dog in it with eyes like mill-wheels; don't mind him. Put him on my apron and help yourself to the money. But if you want as much gold as you can carry, go into the room beyond. The dog sitting on the gold-chest there has eyes like towers! I can tell you that is a dog indeed! He won't do anything to you, however, if you put him on my apron, and then you can take all the gold you want and can carry away.'

'It sounds all right,' said the soldier, 'but what do you want in return?'

'I don't want a penny,' said the witch. 'All I want you to bring me is an old tinder-box that my grandmother left behind when she was down there last.'

'All right, then,' said the soldier. 'Tie the rope round me.'

'There you are,' said the witch. 'And here's my blue apron.'

Then the soldier climbed up the tree, scrambled through the hole, and let himself down into the hall, where, as the witch had said, all those candles were burning. Then he opened the first door. Ah, there sat the dog with eyes like saucers, glaring at him.

'Good dog!' said the soldier, lifting him on to the witch's apron. Then he filled his pockets with coppers, closed the chest, put the dog back, and went into the next room. There, right enough, sat a dog with eyes as big as mill-wheels.

'Please don't stare at me like that,' said the soldier. 'You'll hurt your eyes.' And then he put the dog on the witch's apron. When he saw all the silver in the chest he emptied the coppers out of his pockets, and filled them, and his knapsack, with silver. And then he went into the third room. That was terrible! The dog there really had eyes like

He lifted the dog on to the floor

towers, and his head was turning round like the sails of a windmill.

'Good evening!' said the soldier, raising his cap,

for he had never seen a dog like that; but when he had looked at him carefully he thought, 'It's all right,' and lifted him on to the floor and opened the chest. What heaps of gold! There was enough to buy a whole town and all the sweets, all the tin-soldiers, all the whips and all the rocking-horses in the world! Gold, sure enough!

The soldier threw out all the silver from his knapsack and his pockets and filled them so full of

The witch pulled him up

12

gold coins, and his cap and his boots too, that he could hardly move. Then he put the dog back on the chest, closed the door of the room behind him, and shouted up the tree, 'Pull me up now, old witch!'

'Have you got the tinder-box?' asked the witch.

'Upon my word I'd forgotten it,' said the soldier, and he went and got it. Then the witch pulled him up, and there he was on the road again, with his pockets, his boots, his knapsack and his cap full of gold pieces.

'What do you want the tinder-box for?' asked the soldier.

'That's nothing to do with you,' said the witch. 'You've got the money; give me the tinder-box.'

'Not so fast,' said the soldier. 'If you don't tell me what you want it for I'll draw my sword and cut your head off.'

'I won't tell you,' said the witch.

So the soldier cut her head off. There she lay! He put all his gold into her apron, and slung it over his shoulder. Then, with the tinder-box in his pocket, he went on his way into the town.

It was a fine town, and he took the best room in the best inn, and ordered his favourite dinner, for wasn't he rich? The servant who cleaned his boots thought it a pity that a man so rich should have such an old pair, for as yet he hadn't bought any new ones; next day, however, he got some good boots and grand clothes. So now the soldier was a fine gentleman, and he heard all the society news of the town, and about the King, and what a darling his daughter was.

'Where is she to be seen?' asked the soldier.

'Nobody ever sees her,' he was told. 'She lives in a big castle, surrounded by towers and walls. Nobody but the King goes in and out, because it has been foretold that she will marry a plain soldier and the King won't have that.'

'How I should like to see her!' thought the soldier, but he could not get leave to do so.

He lived a very jolly life; went to the theatre, drove in the royal park and gave lots of money to the poor. He really enjoyed himself, for he remembered what it was like to be without a penny. While his money and his fine clothes lasted he had plenty of fine friends who said he was a wonderful fellow, a real nobleman, and that pleased the soldier very much, but as he was always spending and never earning there came a day when he had nothing left but two farthings. He had to give up his fine room and move into a tiny attic, and clean and patch his own boots.

His fine friends didn't visit him any more—there were too many steps to climb. One dark evening, when he could not afford to buy even a candle, he remembered that there was still a bit of one in the tinder-box which he had brought out of the hollow tree. He thought he would use it up, but the moment he tried to strike a light the door sprang open and there stood the dog with eyes as big as saucers, asking him, 'What are your orders?'

'What do you say?' asked the soldier. 'This is a fine tinder-box if this is the way to get anything I want! Get me some money,' he said to the dog, and in an instant it had gone and come back with a big purse of gold in its mouth.

Then the soldier understood what a wonderful tinder-box it was. If he struck once, it brought the dog which sat on the chest of coppers; twice, and there came the one that guarded the silver; thrice, and the one with the gold arrived. He was able to return to his grand room; he wore good clothes again, and once more he had fine friends who flattered him.

15

Then this thought came into his head. 'It's very strange that the Princess is not to be seen. She is said to be very pretty, but what's the good of that when she's always in the big castle with the towers? Can't I manage to see her? Where's my tinder-box?' He struck the flint, and there stood the dog with eyes like saucers.

'I know it's very late,' said the soldier, 'but I do want to see the Princess for a moment.'

The dog was gone, and before the soldier had had time to think it had returned with the Princess asleep on its back. She was so lovely that anyone could see she was a real Princess. What could a real soldier do but give her a kiss?

The dog brings
back the Princess

Gave lots of money to the poor

(SEE P. 14)

Then the dog ran back with her. In the morning the Princess told the King and Queen that she had had a wonderful dream about a dog and a soldier. She had ridden on the dog's back and the soldier had kissed her.

'That's a fine tale!' said the Queen.

The next night an old lady-in-waiting watched by the Princess's bed to find out what it all meant.

The soldier had a great longing to see the Princess again, so back came the dog, and took her and ran off as fast as it could go, but the old lady-in-waiting ran after it just as fast. When she saw the dog with the Princess go into a large house, she thought, 'Now I know where she is,' and made a big cross with chalk on the door. Then she went home, and the dog returned with the Princess. But when it saw that a cross had been chalked on the door of the house where the soldier lived, it got a piece of chalk too and made a cross on every door in the town! That was clever, for the old lady-in-waiting wouldn't be able to find the right door, because crosses were on them all.

Early in the morning, the King and Queen, with the old lady-in-waiting, and a lot of officials, went to see where the Princess had been.

'It was there!' said the King, seeing a door with a cross on it.

'There, my dear,' said the Queen, for there was another door with the same mark.

'Or there, or there, or there!' said the others; wherever they looked there were chalked crosses on the doors. So it was clear that the hunt was in vain.

Now the Queen was a clever woman who could do a great deal more than just ride in a coach. With her big golden scissors she cut up a piece of silk and made a neat little bag which she filled with white flour. This she fastened on to the Princess's back, and made a tiny hole in it, so that the flour would leave a trail wherever she went.

During the next night the dog came again, took the Princess on its back and ran off with her to the soldier, who had fallen in love with her and wished he had been a Prince so that she might have married him.

The dog did not notice the trail of flour all the way from the palace, so in the morning the King and Queen knew where the Princess had been, and they put the soldier in prison.

There he sat. How dark and horrible it was, and

into the bargain he was told, 'You will be hanged tomorrow.' That wasn't pleasant to hear, and he had left the tinder-box in his room. In the morning he could see through the iron-barred window how everybody was hurrying to see him hanged. He heard trumpets and saw soldiers marching. Amongst the crowd was a shoemaker's apprentice with his leather apron, and wearing slippers. He was running so fast that one of his slippers flew off and hit the wall close to the window where the soldier was looking out.

'Hi, young shoemaker! You've no need to be in such a hurry,' said the soldier. 'Nothing will happen till I come. If you'll run to the inn where I was staying and bring me my tinder-box, I'll give you a shilling. But you must be quick.'

The shoemaker's apprentice wanted the shilling, and he made haste to bring the tinder-box to the soldier—and now something is sure to happen!

Outside the town a tall gallows had been built, and round it stood the soldiers and thousands of people. The King and Queen were there, sitting on a splendid throne, and opposite them the Judges and the Councillors.

Already the soldier was standing on the ladder

'Save me from being hanged!'

leading up to the gallows, but as the noose was about to be put over his head he said that a poor fellow was always allowed one harmless favour before he was executed. He would like to smoke a pipe for the last time.

The King couldn't refuse that, so the soldier

'How would you like to exchange?'

(SEE P. 24)

took out his tinder-box and struck the flint once, twice, thrice! There stood the three dogs, the first with eyes like saucers, the second with eyes like mill-wheels, and the third with eyes like towers!

'Save me from being hanged!' said the soldier, and the dogs seized the Judges and the Councillors —some by the leg, some by the nose!—and threw them so high in the air that when they came down they were all broken to pieces.

'I won't have——' said the King, but the biggest dog seized him and then the Queen and threw the one after the other. That frightened the guards and the people shouted, 'Good soldier, you shall be our King and shall marry the beautiful Princess!'

Then they put him in the royal coach, and the three dogs jumped round it shouting 'Hurrah!' and the boys whistled on their fingers and the soldiers presented arms. The Princess came from the castle and was made Queen, which she liked very much. The wedding feast lasted eight days, and the dogs sat at table, and their eyes were big with wonder!

WHAT THE OLD MAN DOES IS ALWAYS RIGHT

I'm going to tell you a story I heard when I was a little boy. Every time I think about the story it seems better. Some stories are like some people—they improve with age.

Perhaps you have seen in the country an old farm-house with plants and moss growing on its thatched roof, and with swallows' nests under the eaves. The walls are sloping, and only one of the little windows can open. The branches of the elder-tree hang over the fence, and beneath it is a pool with a few ducks. There is a dog that barks at everything and everybody.

In that sort of house once lived an old farmer and his old wife. They were poor, yet they had one thing that was no use to them—an old horse that got its food by grazing at the roadside. The farmer sometimes rode to town on it or lent it to a neighbour, who would do the old couple a favour in return. Still, it would have been a sensible plan to sell it or exchange it for something they really needed, but what should it be?

'You'll know best, old man,' said the farmer's wife to him. 'This is market-day; ride into town and either sell the horse or make a good exchange. Whatever you do I shall be satisfied. Off with you to market.'

So she put his necktie on for him in a beautiful double bow, brushed his hat round and round with her hand, and gave him a kiss. Then off he went with the horse which was to be sold or exchanged. The old man understood quite well what he was to do.

The sun was hot; not a cloud was in the sky; lots of people were walking or riding to market along the dusty road. There was no shade anywhere.

Amongst the crowd was a man leading a cow to market, as fine a cow as you ever saw.

'She must give lovely milk,' thought the old man. 'What a good exchange that would be—a cow for a horse!'

'Hullo, you with the cow!' he said. 'What do you think of this? A horse is worth more than a cow, but I don't care; a cow would be more use to me. How would you like to exchange?'

'I'll gladly do that,' said the man, so they exchanged.

The farmer might well have gone home then, for he had done what he set out to do, but as he had started for the market he went on, just for the sake of seeing it.

Presently, as he walked on with his cow, he came upon a man driving a sheep. It was a fine sheep, fat and with a thick fleece.

'I should very much like that,' said the farmer. 'It would find plenty of grass along our hedge, and in winter we could keep it in the kitchen. It would

'*Withered apples,*' answered the lad

(SEE P. 27)

most certainly be better to have a sheep than a cow.'

'Shall we exchange?'

The man was quite willing, so now the farmer went on with a sheep.

Soon he noticed a man coming out of a field with a big goose under his arm.

'Heavy, isn't it? A grand plump bird! How well it would look on our pond! My old woman would like it—it could eat scraps. She's often wished she had a goose, and here's the chance; she shall!'

'A grand plump bird!'

'Shall we exchange? I'll be very glad to give you this sheep for that goose.'

The other man had no objection, so our farmer now had a goose.

By this time he was quite near the town. The road was more crowded than ever with people and cattle; they were walking on the footpaths and even on a potato-patch at the roadside where there was a hen. It was tied by one leg so that if it got frightened it couldn't run away.

It had a bright eye and looked altogether a very clever fowl. 'Cluck! Cluck!' it said; what it meant by that there is no knowing, but when our farmer saw it he said, 'That's the finest fowl I've ever seen —finer even than the parson's broody hen. I really must have it. A fowl can always pick up food for itself. It would be a good bargain if I could get it for this goose.'

'Will you exchange?' he asked the owner.

'Exchange? Not a bad idea.'

So they did exchange.

The farmer had done a good deal on his way to town, and he was hot and tired, so when he came near an inn he thought he would have something to eat and drink. As he was going in he met a lad coming out carrying a sack filled with something.

'What have you got in that sack?' the farmer asked.

'Withered apples,' answered the lad. 'For the pigs.'

'That's surely a waste. I wish my old woman at home could see them. Last year there was only one apple on our tree. It stood on our cupboard till it was useless. "It's always property!" my old woman would say. Here she could see something like property—a whole sackful! Yes, I should like her to see that.'

'What would you give for the sackful?' asked the lad.

'What would I give? This hen.' So he handed over the hen, and went into the inn with his apples, putting them down by the stove. The stove was hot, but he didn't worry about that.

A lot of other people were there, horse-dealers and herdsmen, and two foreign travellers so rich that their pockets were almost bursting with money. And they could bet, as you will hear.

Suddenly there was a sound from the stove. The apples were frizzling.

'What's that?'

'Well, you see——' began the farmer, and he told the whole story.

'You'll catch it from your old woman, when you get home,' said one of the foreigners.

'Not I!' said he. 'She'll kiss me and say, "Whatever the old man does is right!"'

'Let's have a bet on it. How much?'

'A sackful of money against my sack will be enough,' said the farmer, 'but I'll add my wife and myself for good measure.'

'Fine! First-rate!' So the bet was made.

In a carriage belonging to the inn the farmer and the two foreigners drove back to his home.

'Good evening, old lady!'

'Good evening, old man!'

'I made the exchange!'

'I made the exchange!'

What the Old Man Does is always Right

'Oh yes, you know your business!' said she, and gave him a hug, paying no heed either to the visitors or the sack.

'I exchanged the horse for a cow.'

'Thank goodness! Now we shall have our own milk and butter and cheese.'

'Oh, but I exchanged the cow for a sheep.'

'All the better,' said his wife. 'You think of everything. We shall have sheep's milk and sheep's cheese and wool for stockings and coats. That is more than we could get from a cow, which would just keep losing its hair. Yes, you think of everything.'

'But I exchanged the sheep for a goose.'

'So we shall really have roast goose this year, you dear old thing! You're always thinking of something to give me pleasure. The goose can walk about and get fat before we roast it.'

'But I exchanged the goose for a hen.'

'A hen! What a good exchange!' his wife said again. 'The fowl will lay eggs and hatch them, and soon we shall have a regular poultry farm. That's a thing I've always longed for.'

'Yes, but I exchanged the hen for a sack of withered apples.'

'What? I really must give you a kiss!' exclaimed his wife. 'My darling little husband! Let me tell you something. When you had gone this morning I began to think what I could give you for supper. An omelet with herbs? I've got eggs and I've got bacon, but no herbs. So I went over to the schoolmaster's. They've got herbs, but his wife is a mean thing though she does pretend to be so sweet. "Can you lend me a handful of herbs?" I said. "Lend?" said she. "No, there's not a thing in our garden, not even a withered apple." And now I could lend her a whole sackful! I could die of laughing!'

And with that she gave him a smacking kiss.

'I like that!' said the two travellers together. 'Things go from bad to worse and they get cheerier! That's well worth our money.'

So they handed over a sackful of gold to the farmer who had been kissed instead of being scolded.

Yes, it always pays when a wife thinks and says that her husband knows best and always does the right thing.

That's my story. I heard it first when I was a child, and now you've heard it too and know that what the old man does is always right.

THE DARNING-NEEDLE

There was once a darning-needle who thought she was fine enough to be a sewing-needle.

'Take care to hold me firmly!' said the darning-needle to the fingers which picked her up. 'Don't let me go! If you drop me, I'm so slender that it's doubtful if anybody could find me.'

'That's all right,' said the fingers, taking her round the middle.

'Notice that I have an attendant,' said the darning-needle, drawing a long piece of thread after her.

The fingers were using the darning-needle to mend a pair of the cook's old slippers.

'This work is not good enough for me,' said the darning-needle. 'I shall never get through. I'm breaking! I'm breaking!'—and she broke. 'Didn't I tell you I was too fine?'

'Now she's useless,' thought the fingers, but they had to keep hold of her, for the cook made her a head out of sealing-wax and put her into the front of her dress.

The darning-needle becomes a brooch!

BARBARA C. FREEMAN.

(SEE P. 34) *And they talked about the conceit of others*

The Darning-Needle

'Well, I'm a brooch now!' said the darning-needle. 'I was sure I should win respect. When one is really worth something, it is found out sooner or later.' She smiled to herself—inside, for nobody can see from outside when a darning-needle is smiling!—and looked around as proudly as if she were riding in a coach.

'Are you made of gold?' asked a plain pin which was near her. 'You look beautiful, and you have a head, though it is very small. Take care of it and see that it grows!'

This made the darning-needle so proud that she gave a jump—and jumped right out of the cook's dress into the sink.

'This is travelling,' said the darning-needle, 'but I do hope I shan't get lost.' But lost she was. 'I'm too fine for this world,' she said, 'but I have plenty of sense, which is always something,' and she kept quite cheerful as she was carried down into the gutter.

All sorts of things were floating above her— shavings, straws and scraps of newspaper.

'How they hurry along!' said the darning-needle. 'They don't know what is below them, but I'm here. There goes a shaving thinking of nothing in the world but itself. There's a straw spinning along, don't *you* think so much of yourself, you'll run into a stone! And there's a piece of newspaper; what was on it is forgotten, but how it spreads itself out!

'I'm quite content to stay here. I know what I really am, and here I mean to remain.'

One day she saw something shiny lying near her. It was only a bit of broken glass, but the darning-needle thought it was a diamond, so when she spoke she pretended to be a brooch.

'Are you really a diamond?'

'Something of that kind.'

So each thought the other was something valuable, and they talked about the conceit of others.

'I used to live in a case belonging to a young lady who was a cook,' the darning-needle said. 'She had five fingers on each hand, and oh, the conceit of them! Yet their work was just to lift me out of my case, and hold me and then put me back again.'

'Did they shine?' asked the piece of glass.

'Shine! No,' said the darning-needle, 'but that didn't keep them from being conceited. All five on each hand were brothers, just fingers, and they stood proudly side by side though they were not all the same size. The outside one, the thumb, stuck out from the rest, and he had only one joint in his back, so he could just bow, but he said that nobody could get on without him. The one next him was always pointing at things—the sun, the moon—and he pressed down the pen when writing was to be done. The longest one could look over his head; next to him was one with a golden girdle, and the smallest—the Pinky—did nothing at all and was very proud of it. And between them, with their boasting, they let me drop into the sink.'

'And so we sit here and shine!' said the bit of glass, and then a lot more water came pouring along the gutter and swept the glass away with it.

'He's off!' said the darning-needle, 'and here am I still. I'm too fine, but I'm proud of it, and should be looked up to for it.'

What wonderful thoughts she had! 'I almost think I must be a sunbeam's child! Perhaps the sun is looking for me, here in the water. But I'm so slender that my own mother could hardly see me. If my eye had not been broken off, I could cry—but I wouldn't; crying is not refined.'

One day some poor children came and began

to look in the gutter where they sometimes found old nails and even pennies.

'Oh!' cried one, who had pricked his finger with the darning-needle, 'what a horrid thing!'

'I'm not a horrid thing! I'm a young lady!' said the darning-needle, but nobody heard her. Her sealing-wax head had come off, and she was dull and dirty, but she thought that made her even finer.

'Here's an egg-shell sailing along!' cried the children, and they put the darning-needle into it.

'I'm black and this is white,' said the darning-needle. 'Black and white go very well together. People will see me properly now. If only I'm not sea-sick!'

Well, she wasn't sea-sick.

'It's a great help against sea-sickness to think you are no ordinary person. The finer you are the more you can bear.'

'Crack!' The wheel of a lorry had gone over the egg-shell.

'Oh, what a weight!' said the darning-needle. 'Now I'm really sea-sick!'

But she wasn't, though the lorry-wheel had gone right over her. She lay there all her length—and there let her lie!

BARBARA C. FREEMAN.

(SEE P. 42) *Above them was the sky with all its stars*

THE SHEPHERDESS AND THE CHIMNEY-SWEEP

Have you ever seen an old, old wooden cupboard, covered with carving? A cupboard like that once stood in a sitting-room; it had belonged to somebody's great grandmother, and it was carved all over with roses and tulips, amongst which peered out the heads of stags. In the middle of the door of the cupboard was a very queer figure like a little grinning man with a beard and goat's legs.

The children of the house called him General Goatylegs.

He was always staring at the dear little china shepherdess who stood on a table under a mirror. Her shoes were golden, her frock had red roses all over it, she wore a gold-coloured hat and carried a shepherd's crook, and very pretty she looked. Close to her stood a china chimney-sweep, and though he was all black—except his face, which was clean and rosy-cheeked—he was as charming as any Prince could be. He stood with his ladder quite near the shepherdess, and they had fallen in love with one another.

Not far away stood an old Chinese gentleman, three times as big as they were. He, like them, was made of the finest china, and he could nod his head. He said that he was the shepherdess's great-grandfather, and that she had to obey him. That was what he had told General Goatylegs, who wanted to marry her.

'You can have a husband carved out of real mahogany,' he told her, 'and be the wife of a General. And that cupboard is full of money belonging to him.'

'I won't live in that dark cupboard!' said the little shepherdess, 'and I've heard that he already has eleven wives in it!'

'Well, you can be the twelfth. Tonight, as soon as you hear a noise in the cupboard, you will be married,' said the Chinese, nodding his head, and then he went to sleep.

The little shepherdess cried and turned to her sweetheart. 'Will you come away with me?' she said. 'We can't stay here.'

'I'll do anything you ask,' answered the chimney-sweep. 'We'll go, and I will work hard for you.'

'If only we were safely off the table!' said she.

'I'll do anything you ask'

'I shan't be happy at all till we're far, far away.'

He cheered her up, and showed her a safe way down the carving on the table-leg. His ladder was a help, too, and soon they were on the floor; but suddenly there was a great noise in the cupboard. The carved stags put out their heads farther and waved their horns, and General Goatylegs jumped up and shouted to the old Chinese, 'They're running away! They're running away!'

This frightened them terribly, and they jumped into another cupboard that was standing open. In that cupboard there was a toy theatre, and the play on the stage was all about two unhappy sweethearts just like themselves.

'I can't bear this!' said the shepherdess. 'I must get out of this cupboard!'

So they went out on to the floor again, and there on the table they saw that the old Chinese gentleman was shaking all over with anger.

'He's coming!' cried the little shepherdess, and she fell on her knees in terror.

'I've an idea,' said the chimney-sweep. 'We'll scramble into that vase in the corner and hide amongst the flowers. He'll never look for us there.'

'That won't do,' she said. 'I know that the old Chinese gentleman was once engaged to the vase, and they are still friends. The only thing for us to do is to run right away into the wide world.'

'Are you really brave enough?' asked the chimney-sweep. 'The world is very, very large, and we might never be able to come back here.'

'I *am* brave enough!' she said.

The chimney-sweep saw that she had made up her mind, so he said, 'The way leads right up the chimney; shan't you be frightened to creep right through the fireplace and then all the way up? If

(SEE P. 44) *And they never ceased to love one another*

Up the chimney!

we go there we shall reach the chimney-top, so high that nobody could reach us, and from there we shall be able to see the whole wide world.'

When he had led her to the fireplace, she said, 'How black it is!' but she went through it with him right into the chimney.

'Here we are at the bottom,' said he. 'And look up there! You can see a beautiful star.'

There it shone, as if it were showing them the way. A difficult way it was, but they clung and scrambled upwards and upwards. He helped her and showed her where to place her little china feet, and at last they got right to the very top of the chimney and there they sat down to rest, for they were very tired, as well they might be!

Above them was the sky with all its stars; beneath them the roofs of the city; they could see far off into the wide world all round. The shepherdess had never thought it could be anything like that! She leaned her little head against the chimney-sweep, and sobbed so that the gold paint cracked off her girdle!

'It's too big!' she said. 'I wish I were back on the table under the mirror, and I shan't be happy till I'm there again. I followed you up here into the great world; now you will take me back, if you like me at all.'

The chimney-sweep reminded her about the old Chinese gentleman and General Goatylegs. But she kept on crying, and she kissed her little chimney-sweep so fondly that he had to do what she wanted, though it was silly.

So down the chimney they climbed, and it was neither nice nor easy, but at last they reached the fireplace again, and stood listening, to find out what was going on in the room.

Everything was quiet, but when they looked out,

'He can be put together again'

there was the old Chinese gentleman lying on the floor, broken into three pieces. He had fallen when he tried to chase the runaways.

But General Goatylegs was still in his usual place.

'This is terrible!' said the little shepherdess. 'My grandfather all broken, and it is our fault! I shall never get over it!' And she wrung her little hands.

'He can be put together again,' said the chimney-sweep, 'quite easily. Some glue and a rivet in his neck will make him as good as new, and he'll be quite able to say nasty things to us again.'

'Do you really think so?' said she, and then they crept back to their old place on the table.

'Well, here we are again,' said the chimney-sweep, 'and we might have saved ourselves a lot of trouble.'

'If only my grandfather were mended!' said the shepherdess. 'Will it cost a great deal?'

In any case mended he was, with glue and a rivet in his neck—but he could not nod his head any more.

'Why have you become so stiff in your manners since you were broken?' asked General Goatylegs. 'I don't see any reason for it. Is the little shepherdess going to marry me, or isn't she?'

The chimney-sweep and the little shepherdess looked at the old Chinese gentleman appealingly. They were afraid he would nod his head, but he couldn't, and he didn't like to tell anyone that he had a rivet in his neck. So the young people were left in peace, very pleased about Grandfather's rivet, and they never ceased to love one another till they got broken.

THE PRINCESS AND THE PEA

There was once a Prince who wanted a Princess for his wife, but she must be a *real* Princess. All about the world he travelled looking for one, but in vain. He met many Princesses, but he could never be sure that they were real Princesses. Always there was something which made him doubtful.

So he went back home very sad, because he wanted a real Princess so much.

Then one night, when the weather was terrible with thunder and lightning and rain, somebody knocked at the door, and the King, the Prince's old father, opened it to see who was there.

It was a Princess who stood outside, but oh, what a state she was in after being out in the stormy night! The water was running down from her hair and her clothes, and even out of her shoes; but she said she was a real Princess.

'We'll soon find out!' thought the old Queen to herself, but, without saying anything about that, she took all the bedclothes off the bed, and put a pea in the middle of it. Then on the top of the pea she piled twenty mattresses and twenty eiderdown quilts.

That was what the Princess would have to sleep on.

In the morning they asked if she had had a good night.

'A very bad one!' said she. 'I didn't have a wink of sleep. I can't think what was in the bed. It was something hard, and after lying on it all night I'm black and blue from head to foot.'

Then they knew that she was indeed a real Princess, because she had felt the pea through twenty mattresses and twenty eiderdown quilts.

So the Prince married her, and was sure that he had a real Princess for his wife, and the pea is still amongst the royal treasures, unless somebody has taken it.

Now that's a true story.

THUMBKIN

There was once a poor woman who had no child but who dearly wanted one. So she went to a nice old witch and asked her help. 'The witch gave her a grain of barley and said, 'This isn't just the kind of barley that farmers sow; plant it in a flower-pot, and see what you will see!'

So the woman gave the witch a few pennies, and went home and planted the barley-corn in a pot, and soon there showed a plant with a flower like a tulip-bud.

'What a pretty flower!' said the woman, and she kissed the red and yellow petals. As she did so

47

they opened, and there inside it lay a tiny girl! She was no bigger than your thumb, and for that reason she was called Thumbkin.

For a cradle Thumbkin had a polished walnut-shell. She slept on white violet-petals, with a rose-petal over her. When she was not asleep she played about on the table, where the good woman put a saucer full of water, with flowers round the edge. Thumbkin had a tulip-petal for a boat, and when she rowed across the saucer what a pretty sight it was!

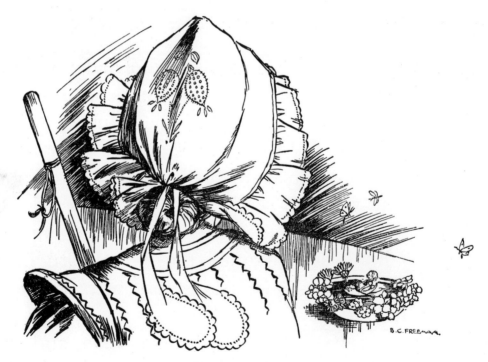

A tulip-petal for a boat

48

'*Plant it in a flower-pot, and see what you will see!*' (SEE P. 47)

Thumbkin

Well, one night when she was fast asleep a big ugly toad came in at the window and hopped down on to the table, and there she saw Thumbkin.

'What a nice wife for my son!' she said, and she picked up the cradle and carried it to the marsh by the river, where she and her son lived.

When he saw Thumbkin all he could say was a croak.

'Don't make so much noise,' said his mother. 'You'll wake her and she might fly away, for she is as light as thistle-down. We will put her on a water-lily leaf in the middle of the river; it will seem like an island to her, and she won't be able to get away.'

So that is what they did, and Thumbkin was left on the leaf in the middle of the river, while Mrs. Toad went to make ready a home for the young people, doing her best to make it pretty with rushes and flowers.

When Thumbkin woke she was frightened and cried, for there was nothing to see all round but water and great big lily-leaves.

By and by Mrs. Toad came back with her son, and said with a bow, 'Here is my son, who is to be your husband; you will live in a fine house under the marsh. It will be a very beautiful home.'

'Croak! Croak!' was still all that her son could say.

The toads thought Thumbkin's walnut-shell cradle would be a fine thing to have in the new house, so they took it away, and left Thumbkin on the lily-leaf without it.

Now the little fish in the river knew all that was going on, and they put their heads out of the water to look at Thumbkin. When they saw what a little darling she was, they made up their minds that she should not marry an ugly toad, and they bit through the stalk of the lily-leaf so that it went floating down the river where the toads could never reach it.

Presently a white butterfly alighted on the leaf. Thumbkin was glad; she took off her little sash and tied one end to the leaf and the other to the butterfly, and off they went down the shining river quicker than ever.

Next came a cockchafer—a handsome brown flying beetle, with wings that looked like rainbows when he moved them fast. He picked up Thumbkin, and flew off with her into a big tree. Thumbkin was afraid, and she was sorry for the butterfly, still tied to the leaf; how would he get any food?

'What an ugly slim waist!'

The cockchafer didn't worry about that. He set her down on the tree, brought her some honey from a flower, and told her that she was pretty, though she was not like a cockchafer.

All the other cockchafers who lived in the tree came to see her, and the cockchafer ladies wagged their feelers and talked about her.

'What a pity she has only two legs!' they said. 'She has no feelers!'

'What an ugly slim waist!'

The first cockchafer really thought she was pretty and liked her very much, but when all the rest said she was ugly, he supposed they were right, and so instead of keeping her he carried her down from the tree and left her sitting on a big daisy, all alone in the wood.

There in the wood she spent the whole summer and autumn, weaving a bed of grasses which she hung under a clover-leaf. For food she had honey from the flowers, and for drink the morning dew.

Then winter came. The birds which had sung to her flew away, the trees lost their leaves, and her clover-leaf withered. Thumbkin was very cold, for by now her clothes were ragged. Snow began to fall, and because she was so tiny, to her every flake was like a whole spadeful of snow to us.

She tried to roll herself up in a dry leaf, but it was no good. Near the forest was a reaped field,

Then winter came

(SEE P. 54)

He showed them where it lay

and there she went wandering amongst the frozen stubble, which was like another wood to her. There she came to the home of Mrs. Fieldmouse, who lived in a cosy little home under the ground, with plenty of grains of barley in her store, and a nice sitting-room, kitchen and dining-room.

Just like any beggar-girl, Thumbkin knocked at the door and asked for a little piece of a barley-grain, because she had had nothing to eat for two whole days.

'You poor little thing!' cried the kind old Fieldmouse. 'Come in and have a meal with me. You can spend the winter here, if you will keep my house tidy and tell me stories.'

Thumbkin agreed to do so, and was well content.

'We are going to have a visitor,' said the Fieldmouse. 'My neighbour comes to see me once a week. He is rich, and wears a fine black fur coat, and he would make a fine husband for you! But he doesn't see very well.'

Well, Thumbkin knew this neighbour was just old Mr. Mole, and she didn't like him very much. Still, she sang her prettiest songs to him, and he fell in love with her because of her sweet voice.

He told the Fieldmouse and Thumbkin that they could use the long passage he had dug between their house and his, and said they need not be afraid of the dead bird which was lying there. It must have been buried, for he found it when he was digging.

He showed them where it lay, and made a hole in the roof of the passage so that the light came in, and they could see that it was a poor swallow that looked as if it had died of the cold.

Thumbkin was sad to see it, for she loved the birds, but the Mole just pushed it aside with his foot and said, 'Well, he won't twitter any more! How wretched to be a bird! They do nothing but twitter and sing, and then in winter they starve.'

'What you say is very wise,' answered the Field-mouse, 'and yet some people admire them.'

Thumbkin said nothing, but when the other two had turned their backs she stooped down to the bird and kissed its closed eyes.

'Perhaps it was you I heard in the summer,' she thought. 'What pleasure you gave me, you pretty thing!'

Mr. Mole stopped up the hole in the roof which he had made, and saw the two ladies home.

Thumbkin

That night, instead of going to sleep, Thumbkin wove a rug of dry hay, and took it along the passage to the bird that was lying there so still. She tucked the rug over him so that he might at least be warm.

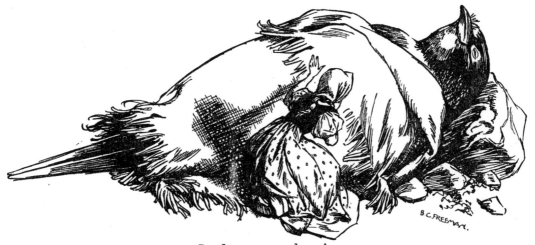

Its heart was beating

'Good-bye, dear bird,' she said, 'and thank you!'

Then, as she laid her head for a moment on its breast, she heard something; its heart was beating; it was not dead! In the autumn, when the other swallows flew away to warm countries, this one had been left behind, and the cold had almost killed it.

Thumbkin was rather frightened, for to her the swallow seemed a giant bird, but she tried to be brave, and wrapped the rug closer round him, and fetched a rose-petal from her own bed and placed it over his head.

The next night the swallow was much better, but still so weak that he could only just open his eyes and look at Thumbkin.

'Thank you, dear child,' he said, 'I shall soon be able to get up and fly about in the sunshine again.'

'Oh!' she said, 'it is too cold now. Stay in your warm bed and I will nurse you.'

She brought him some water in a petal, and when he had drunk a little he told her how he had hurt his wing, so that he could not fly as fast as the others, and how he had fallen to the ground. That was all he knew.

So Thumbkin looked after the swallow all winter, and did not tell Mrs. Fieldmouse or Mr. Mole about him, in case they should be unkind to him.

At last spring came and the earth grew warm, and when Thumbkin opened the hole in the roof of the passage the sun shone in. The swallow wanted her to fly away with him, but she did not like to vex the Fieldmouse by leaving her.

'No, I cannot come,' she said.

Thumbkin's wedding clothes were all ready

'Then, good-bye, you darling,' said the swallow at last, and off he flew, while Thumbkin's eyes were full of tears.

She was not allowed to go walking, and the spring corn was already so high that again the field was like a forest.

'Now it is time you got your wedding clothes ready!' said Mrs. Fieldmouse one day, for the Mole had told her that he wanted to marry Thumbkin.

So Thumbkin had to work hard at the spinning-wheel, and Mrs. Fieldmouse hired four caterpillars, fine spinners, to help her. Every evening the dull old Mole came to call, and to talk about the wedding, which was to take place at the end of the summer.

Poor Thumbkin was unhappy, for she couldn't bear him. Every day, at sunrise and sunset, she went to look out at the front door, and when the wind blew aside the corn-stalks so that she could see the blue sky, she thought of the swallow and wished he would return.

By the time autumn was near, Thumbkin's wedding clothes were all ready.

'You will be married four weeks from now,' Mrs. Fieldmouse told her, but Thumbkin cried, and said she really didn't want to marry Mr. Mole.

'Rubbish!' said the Fieldmouse. 'Don't be so silly or I shall give you a nip with my sharp teeth! He'll make you a fine husband. Even a Queen hasn't such a fine fur coat, and he is really very well-off. You ought to be very thankful.'

Well, the wedding-day came, and Mr. Mole arrived to take Thumbkin away to his house under the earth, where she would never see the sun; it was time to say good-bye to him.

'Good-bye, bright sun!' she said, holding out her arms, and then she clasped round them a little flower and said again, 'Good-bye! Good-bye! Give the swallow my greetings if you see him.'

Suddenly overhead she heard 'Twitter! Twitter!' and there was the swallow. She told him her troubles, and could not help crying.

'Winter is coming,' the swallow said, 'and I am going off to a warm country; won't you come with me? You can tie yourself on to my back with your girdle, and we'll fly far away from that horrid mole and his gloomy house, to a country where the sun always shines and the loveliest flowers grow. You saved my life; come with me, Thumbkin!'

'Yes, I will come with you,' she said, and got

Up into the air he flew

on to his back, where she tied herself to one of his strongest feathers. Then up into the air he flew, over forests and seas and mountains all white with snow. It was cold up there, but Thumbkin snuggled down into the swallow's feathers, with only her little head out so that she could see the wonderful sights below.

Soon they came to warm countries where vines grew and oranges and lemons, and the air was full of sweet scents, and in the lanes children were playing with bright butterflies; but the swallow still flew on till at last he came to an island where, amongst beautiful trees, stood the ruins of a white marble palace.

Swallows had built their nests amongst the tall pillars, and Thumbkin's swallow told her that that was where he lived.

'Choose a flower for your own house,' he said, 'and I will set you down there, and you shall have everything you want.'

'How lovely!' cried Thumbkin, and clapped her little hands. On the ground lay a great pillar which had fallen and broken as it fell, and between the broken pieces were growing the most beautiful white blossoms. The swallow flew down there with Thumbkin, and she stepped off his back on to a broad leaf —and then how surprised she was! In the middle of one of the flowers she saw a tiny prince with a gold crown on his head and shining wings on his shoulders.

He was the Prince of the Flower Elves, and in that flower he lived all alone.

'How handsome he is!' whispered Thumbkin to her swallow.

The Prince was rather afraid of the great bird, but as soon as he saw Thumbkin he was filled with joy, for she was the prettiest little maiden he had ever seen. Taking off his crown, he put it on her head, and asked her what her name was, and said that if she would marry him she should be Queen of the Flower Elves. What a different husband he would be from the toad or the mole with his black velvet coat!

Of course Thumbkin said she would marry him, and then from every flower came a tiny lady or a tiny man, so dainty, it was a treat to see them. Every one brought her a present, and the best present of all was a lovely little pair of wings, which were fastened to her shoulders so that she too could flit about amongst the flowers. There were great rejoicings, and the swallow sat up above in his nest and twittered to them, though he was a little sad because Thumbkin would not be with him any more.

'You shan't be called Thumbkin!' said the Prince to his bride. 'I don't like that name. I shall call you Maia.'

'Good-bye and be happy!' called the swallow when the wedding was over, and he set off to fly back to the north country where he would spend the summer. There he had a nest over the window of a house where lived a man who could tell fairy tales; the swallow twittered to this man, and that is how this story came to be told!

THE SWINEHERD

There was once a poor Prince who had only a very small kingdom, but it was large enough to have a queen, and so he made up his mind to marry.

It was a little bold of him to ask the Emperor's daughter if she would have him, but he did, for his name was famous, and there were hundreds of princesses who would have said yes. We shall see what the Emperor's daughter said.

On the grave of the Prince's father there grew a rose tree. It bloomed only once a year, and then bore only one flower, but that one rose was so sweet that anyone who smelled it forgot all his

62

troubles. The Prince had also a nightingale which sang as if all music were in its throat. The rose and the nightingale were to be presents for the Princess, and they were sent to her in two big silver caskets.

They were brought in while the Emperor was sitting in the great hall, where the Princess and her ladies were playing a game called 'Somebody's Coming'. When she saw the big caskets she cried, 'I do hope he has sent me a dear little kitten!' but the lovely rose was unpacked.

'How cleverly it is made!' said one of the ladies.

'It is more than clever,' said the Emperor, 'it is beautiful.'

But when the Princess touched it she was ready to weep. 'Oh, Father,' she cried, 'it isn't a work of art at all, it's natural!'

'What!' cried the ladies. 'Just natural?'

'Well, let us see what is in the other casket, before we get angry,' said the Emperor, and there was the nightingale singing so beautifully that nobody could find any fault with it. The ladies praised it in French. They liked to chatter in French!

'The bird's singing reminds me of the late Empress's musical box,' said an old courtier. 'It has the same tone, the same expression.'

'You are right,' said the Emperor, and he cried like a child.

'Let's hope it isn't just a living bird!' said the Princess.

'That's what it is,' said the messenger who had brought it.

'Then set it free,' said the Princess, and she wouldn't see the Prince.

He wasn't going to be got rid of like that, however. He stained his face brown, pulled his hat over his eyes, and knocked at the door.

'Good day, Emperor!' he said. 'Can I get any work here at the castle?'

'Certainly,' said the Emperor. 'I want somebody to look after the pigs.'

So the Prince became the Emperor's swineherd. He was given a wretched little hut amongst the pig-styes, but all day he sat working, and by evening he had made a little saucepan that had little bells all round it, and when something was being cooked in the saucepan all the bells tinkled and played the tune of an old song:

> 'Ah, my darling Augustine,
> Everything is over!'

But the most wonderful thing about the saucepan

'Let's hope it isn't just a living bird!'

was that whoever put his finger into the steam rising from it knew what was being cooked on every fire in the city.

As the Princess and her ladies were walking along she heard the tune, and was delighted, because it was the only music she could play, and that with one finger.

'He's doing what I can!' she said. 'He must be an educated swineherd. Go and ask him what is the price of his instrument.'

So, putting on a pair of clogs, one of the ladies went to the pig-styes and talked to him.

'What will you take for that saucepan?' asked the lady.

'Ten kisses from the Princess!' said he.

'What ever next!' cried she.

'That's my price,' replied the swineherd.

'What insolence!' said the Princess when she heard, and she walked on—but the music was so pretty!

'Ah, my darling Augustine,
  Everything is over!"

'Ask him if ten kisses from my ladies will do, said the Princess.

'Thank you,' said the swineherd, 'but—ten

kisses from the Princess, or I don't part with my saucepan.'

'Bother!' said the Princess. 'All stand round me so that nobody can see.'

So the swineherd had the ten kisses and the Princess had the saucepan. What fun it was! The saucepan was cooking something all day long, and the Princess knew what everybody in the town was going to have for dinner.

The swineherd-prince was never idle, and one day he made a rattle which, when it was whirled round, played all sorts of dance-music.

The rattle played dance-music

The Swineherd

'Marvellous!' said the Princess when she heard it. 'Ask him what he wants for it—but no more kisses, mind!'

'He wants a hundred kisses from the Princess,' she was told.

'He's mad!' said she, but then she thought again and said, 'I'm the Emperor's daughter, and I must encourage art. Tell him I'll give him ten kisses and my ladies will give him the rest.'

'We don't want to kiss him!' they cried.

'Nonsense!' said the Princess. 'If I can kiss him, you can and must.'

But when they told him what she had said he replied, 'A hundred kisses from the Princess, or I shan't part with this rattle.'

'Well, gather round me!' said the Princess, and her ladies did as they were told.

'What's going on there, amongst the pig-styes?' thought the Emperor, looking down from a balcony. He rubbed his eyes and put on his glasses, and then hurried down.

He went very quietly, and the ladies were so taken up counting the kisses that they did not know he was coming. He was just in time to box his daughter's ears at the eighty-sixth kiss.

'Away with you!' he cried, for he was very angry, and he ordered both the Princess and the swineherd to leave the kingdom.

So there she was, crying, and the rain came pouring down!

'Oh, how unlucky I am!' said the Princess. 'Why didn't I accept that handsome Prince!'

Meanwhile the swineherd had gone behind a tree, rubbed the stain off his face, and thrown away his rags; and now he stepped out in all his royal array, looking so fine that she had to bow before him.

'I've learned to despise you,' he said. 'You wouldn't have an honest Prince. You thought the rose and the nightingale were worthless, but you were willing to kiss a swineherd for a toy. Now see what you have earned!'

And off he went, home to his own kingdom, while she might well have sung:

'Ah, my darling Augustine,
Everything is over!'

'Well, gather round me!' said the princess (SEE P. 67)

THE SIX SWANS

A King one day went hunting in the forest, and he chased a deer so far and fast that nobody could keep up with him. When evening came, he halted and looked around to see where he was, and knew that he was lost. He looked in vain for a way out of the woods. Then he saw an old woman sitting in a hollow tree: she was a witch.

'My good woman,' he said to her, 'can you show me a way out of the woods?"

'I can easily do that, O King,' she answered,

'but on one condition. If you don't agree to it you'll never get out, but will die of hunger here.'

'And what is the condition?' asked the King.

'I have a daughter,' said the old woman; 'she is very beautiful and worthy to be your wife. If you will make her your Queen I will show you the way out of the wood.'

The King, in his distress, agreed, and the old woman took him to her hut, where her daughter, who was sitting by the fire, welcomed the King as if she had expected him. Beautiful indeed she was, and yet he could not look at her without

Beautiful indeed she was

horror. When he had lifted her on to his horse, the old woman showed him the path, and by and by he reached the royal castle, where the wedding took place.

Now the King had been married before, and his first wife had left him seven children, six boys and a girl, whom he loved more than anything else in the world. As he was afraid that their stepmother might treat them badly and do them harm, he took them to a lonely castle in the middle of a forest. It was in such a secret place that he would not himself have been able to find it, had not a wise woman given him a ball of magic yarn; when he threw it down before him, it unwound itself and led the way.

Well, the King visited his dear children so often that his wife noticed it, and grew inquisitive to know what he was doing in the woods. So she paid his servants a lot of money to tell her the secret, and they told her also about the magic yarn. After that she had no rest till she knew where the King hid the ball. Then she made little white shirts of silk, and as she had learned witchcraft from her mother, she sewed a spell into each.

One day, when the King had gone hunting, she

took the shirts and went into the wood, with the ball of yarn to show her the way. When the boys heard somebody coming, they thought it was their dear father, and ran joyfully to meet him. Then she threw one of the little shirts over each, and as soon as it touched him he turned into a swan which flew away over the forest.

She went home pleased to think she had got rid of her stepchildren, but the girl had not run out with her brothers, and the Queen knew nothing about her.

Next day, when the King went to visit his children, he found only the little girl.

'Where are your brothers?' he asked.

'Oh, father dear,' she answered, 'they have gone away and left me alone,' and she told him how from her little window she had seen her brothers turn into swans and fly off over the trees, and showed him the feathers which they had let fall in the courtyard, and which she had picked up.

The King was full of sorrow, but he never guessed that this was the Queen's wicked work, and as he feared lest the little girl also should be stolen away, he made up his mind to take her with him: but she was afraid of her stepmother, and

(SEE P. 74)

'Can't you be set free anyhow?'

begged her father to leave her for one more night in the castle in the woods.

For the poor little girl thought to herself: 'This is no place for me to stay. I shall go off to seek my brothers,' and when night came she fled away into the forest. She kept on walking all night and the next day till she was too tired to go any farther, and when she came to a hut, she went in and found a room with six little beds in it. She didn't like to lie down on any of them, but instead crept underneath one, to spend the night on the hard floor. Just before sunset she heard a rushing of wings, and then six swans flew in at the window. They settled down on the floor and blew upon one another, and blew all the feathers off, and their swan-skins came off like shirts.

The little girl watched, and recognized her brothers, and joyfully crept out from under the bed. When her brothers saw her, they were as happy as she, but their happiness did not last long.

'You mustn't stay here,' they told her. 'This is a robbers' hut, and when they come back they will kill you.'

'Can't you protect me?' asked their little sister.

'No,' they answered, 'for we can take off our

swan-shirts and appear as ourselves for only a quarter of an hour every evening, then we are turned back into swans.'

Their little sister cried and asked, 'Can't you be set free anyhow?'

'Ah, no,' they replied, 'the conditions are too difficult—for six years you would have neither to speak nor smile, and during that time make us six shirts out of daisies. If you spoke one single word, all the work would go for nothing.'

No sooner had her brothers told her this than the quarter of an hour was over, and off they flew through the window, swans again.

Then the little girl made a great resolve: she would set her brothers free though it should cost her her life! She left the hut, went out into the forest, and spent the night sitting in a tree. In the morning she gathered daisies and began to sew them together. She must not speak to anybody: she did not feel like smiling: she just sat there in the tree and worked.

It happened that the King of that country was hunting in the woods, and after the little girl had been sitting there for a long time, his huntsmen came to the tree where she sat. One shouted to her,

'Who are you?' but she gave no answer. 'Come down,' they called, 'we won't hurt you.' She only shook her head. As they kept on troubling her with questions, she took off her golden necklace and threw it down to them, hoping they would be content to have that and go away. Then, as they kept on questioning, she threw down her jewelled girdle, and one by one all her fine things till she had nothing left but her plain smock.

Even then the huntsmen wouldn't go away: they climbed the tree, carried her down, and took her to the King.

'Come down, we won't hurt you'

The King asked her, 'Who are you? What were you doing up in the tree?' but she gave no reply.

He questioned her in all the languages he knew, but she kept as dumb as a fish.

Now she was very pretty, and the King was falling in love with her, so he wrapped her in his cloak, placed her before him on his horse, and took her home to his castle. There she was dressed in splendid garments, so that her beauty shone like a sunny day, but not one word would she speak.

She sat at the King's side at table, and her fine manners and noble air so pleased him that he said, 'This is she I mean to marry, and no other girl in the world,' and the wedding took place a few days later.

But the King's mother was wicked: she did not like the marriage and talked against the young Queen.

'Who knows anything about the chit?' she said. 'She can't speak: she's not worthy of the King.'

When a year later the first royal baby was born, the wicked old woman took it away and told the King that the Queen had killed it. This the King would not believe, and he would not allow any harm to be done to his wife. Meanwhile she sat

The wicked mother-in-law played the same trick

silent as before and went on sewing just as calmly.

The following year another baby was born, a beautiful boy. The wicked mother-in-law played the same trick, but still the King couldn't bring himself to believe her story.

'My Queen is too good and gentle,' he said, 'to do such a thing, and if she were not dumb she would prove her innocence.'

But when, for the third time, the old woman took away a new-born baby and accused the Queen, who spoke not a word to defend herself, the King could do nothing but send her before the judges, who condemned her to be burned.

Now the day on which she was to die was the very last day of the six years in which she was not to speak or to smile, and so she had saved her dear brothers from the spell. The six shirts were finished all but the left sleeve of the last.

When the time came for her to be driven to the place where she must die, she put the six shirts over her arm, and then, when the fire was about to be lit, she looked all around, and there came six swans speeding through the air!

So she knew that the hour of their freedom had come, and her heart swelled with joy.

The swans dived down to her and drew so close that she was able to throw the shirts over them: and all, as the shirts touched them, threw off the likeness of swans and stood up before her, gay and handsome. (Only the youngest lacked a left arm: a swan's wing rose from his shoulder instead.)

They kissed and petted their sister, who went to the King and told him everything. 'Dearest husband, at last I may speak and make you understand that I am not guilty, but falsely accused,' and she told the King of the old woman's trick, and how it was she who had taken away the babies and hidden them. And to the King's great joy they were brought back. The wicked old woman was condemned to be burned to ashes, and the King and Queen and her six brothers lived many many years in peace and happiness.

THE EMPEROR'S NEW CLOTHES

Many a year ago there was an Emperor so fond of fine clothes that all his money was spent on them. He had a different suit for every hour in the day. When anybody asked where he was, the answer would not be, 'With his wise Counsellors in the Council Chamber,' but, 'In his dressing-room.'

One day there came to the city two rascals who said that they were weavers who could weave cloth not only very beautiful, but with something very strange about it; those who were not doing their work properly, and very stupid people, could not even see it!

'A suit of that kind,' thought the Emperor, 'would be the very thing for me! It would help me to know whether my servants were doing their work, and who were the really stupid ones.'

So the cunning pair were ordered to make one of their wonderful suits for his Highness. Money was given them, and the finest silk to weave, and gold lace. These they kept for themselves, but they set up two weaving-machines, and sat at them day and night pretending to be very busy, though there was

'What a pattern! What colours!'

no silk at all on the machines at which they worked.

After a time the Emperor thought he would like to know how the cloth for his new suit was getting on, and sent the Prime Minister to find out.

When the Prime Minister looked at the weaving-machines and saw, of course, nothing being woven, he was horrified.

'Does this mean that I am not doing my duty?' he asked himself—'that I am stupid?'

So when the rascals asked how he liked their work, he exclaimed, 'Marvellous! What a pattern!' What colours!'

As the weavers described the pattern, and

'*Nobody ever had such fine clothes as our emperor!*' (SEE P. 84)

BARBARA C. FREEMAN.

pointed to the colours they pretended to be using, he took care to remember all they said, so that he could repeat it to the Emperor, which he did.

Pleased to know that they were getting on so well, the Emperor sent yet more money and fine silk and gold lace to the weavers, who went on busily weaving nothing! When another statesman was sent to report, he did just the same as the Prime Minister. It would never do to let anybody know that he could not even see the magic cloth, and so prove that he was not doing his work and that he was stupid!

Soon everybody in the city was talking about the clothes that were being made for the Emperor, and what it meant if anybody could not see them.

One day the Emperor, taking some of his wisest men, with the Prime Minister and the other statesmen who had visited the weavers, went to see the marvellous cloth for himself.

'Isn't it splendid?' said the two who had been before, and were ready with their words, and they repeated what the two rogues had said. 'Look at this crimson and this gold! Look at the pattern, here, and here,' and they pointed at what was not there.

'Well, *I* can't see anything at all! Am I stupid? Am I not fit to be Emperor?' That was what the Emperor thought, but what he said was, 'My imperial opinion is that it is really beautiful.'

After bowing graciously to the two rogues, he stood gazing, as if delighted, at the empty weaving-machines.

All the great people with him nodded their heads and agreed. 'Beautiful, indeed, your Highness!' they said, and they got the Emperor to promise that he would wear the new clothes on the great public holiday which was soon to take place.

To show how pleased he was with their work, the Emperor gave the two rogues a medal each, with permission to call themselves 'Weavers to the Court'.

The night before the holiday the rascals sat late in their lighted workshop, and passers-by could see how busy they were, with their arms and fingers moving as if they were using needle and thread and big scissors, like a pair of tailors hard at work.

Early in the morning came the Emperor with all his Counsellors and courtiers, to have the new clothes fitted on, and the two scamps kept up the pretence.

The Emperor's New Clothes

'Here are the breeches,' they said, as if holding them up. 'This is the coat, and this the cloak with its train. Note how light they all are, your Highness. You will scarcely feel any weight at all.'

'Perfectly true!' cried all the courtiers.

'Will your Highness be pleased to try them on?' said the weavers, and the Emperor pretended he was being dressed, while they helped him, acting as if they were picking up one garment after another and putting it on their Imperial customer.

'How well they fit!' cried the courtiers. 'How perfectly they suit your Highness!'

'The procession is drawn up outside,' said an official, 'only waiting for your Highness to take your place at its head.'

'I am ready,' the Emperor answered, turning to have one more look at himself in the big looking-glass, as a man does when he is going out in a new suit for the first time.

Then the pages, whose duty it was to carry the train of the Emperor's cloak, stooped down and acted as though they were lifting something from the ground. They did not want, any more than the rest, that anybody should know they could not see any train to carry!

So out into the street went the Emperor, his train-bearers, Counsellors and courtiers. Taking their places at the head of the procession, off they marched through the cheering crowds.

Everybody had heard about the new clothes, and that they could not be seen by those who were stupid or who were not doing their work properly, so that on every side rose cries of admiration.

'Nobody ever had such fine clothes as our Emperor!'

'What a grand train!'

'How fine he looks dressed like that!'

Then suddenly a little boy's voice was heard above the rest, saying loudly:

'But he hasn't any clothes on at all!'

'That's what a child thinks!' said his father, but the people around began to repeat what the youngster had said, first in whispers, then louder, till all the crowds were shouting:

'He hasn't any clothes on!'

It seemed to the Emperor that they were right, but he said to himself, 'I mustn't seem to agree with them,' so on he marched, and the pages marched behind him, still holding up the train of the cloak that wasn't there!